The Jung

by Tracey P

Adapted from the novel by Rudyard Kipling

Baker's Plays
7611 Sunset Blvd.
Los Angeles, CA 90042
bakersplays.com

NOTICE

THE JUNGLE BOOK was first produced by Geordie Productions in Montreal, Canada. The performance was directed by Dean Patrick Fleming, with sets by Amy Keith, costumes by Susana Vera, and lighting by Ana Cappelluto. The Production Stage Manager was Melanie St Jacques. The cast was as follows:

MOWGLI.....................................Oliver Koomsatira

BALOO/MONKEY KING.........................Harry Standjofski

BAGHEERA/FATHER WOLF/MONKEY..............Quincy Armorer

SHERE KHAN....................................Chip Chuipka

TABAQUI/MONKEY............................Glenda Braganza

RAKSHA/AKELA/MONKEY.........................Paula Hixson

PERCUSSIONIST................................Kristie Ibrahim

NOTES ABOUT CASTING
AND CONCEPT

The Jungle Book is to be performed by an ensemble of at least five performers. It should consist of one actor to play Mowgli, and two women and two men to play all the other characters. An onstage musician will provide the soundscape for the production. A percussionist was used for the premiere production.

Sample Casting Breakdown

Actor 1: Baloo - Monkey King - Human, Shere Khan
Actor 2: Bagheera - Father Wolf - Monkey 3, Shere Khan
Actor 3: Mowgli - Young Mowgli Puppeteer
Actress 1: Raksha - Akela - Kaa - Monkey 2
Actress 2: Tabaqui - Monkey 1

If using a cast of 5: In Scene 11, Baloo will need to take Bagheera's lines while that actor plays Shere Khan.

The monkeys and humans are in masks, and all other characters can be created using either masks or puppets. Besides Kaa and Rann, any puppets should allow the actor to use his/her own movement to portray the animals body.

Kaa the rock snake had an oversized head and a long winding body. Rann can be a kite type bird on the top of a bamboo stick. Young Mowgli is a puppet of a two year-old boy.

The actors will play multiple characters. Actors will also assist in the vocals/sounds of the soundscape along with the musician. The actors should have strong movement, and vocal skills. While *The Jungle Book* is not a typical musical or dance piece it is meant to contain elements of movement and song that resonate the Indian jungle that inspired Rudyard Kipling.

THE MUSIC

Depending on what instruments are being played by the productions' musician, the music for *The Jungle Book* can be creatively interpreted by the Director. Some things to keep in mind are *The Law of the Jungle* is written in the style of beat poetry for Baloo, it does not need to be sung but set to rhythm. The music for the lullaby, *Jungle Favour* has been included with the script and was originally performed with drum accompaniment and in a subsequent production with ukulele.

The Monkey Song was originally performed in the style of beat poetry with drum accompaniment and in the subsequent production was sung and accompanied by banjo and kazoo. The music for *The Monkey Song* written by Steven Charles is available by emailing the author at traceypower@shaw.ca.

Special thanks for the script development assistance of Brian Dooley, the Citadel Theatre Play Development Program, Geordie Productions and Playwright's Workshop Montreal. Special thanks also to my family for their incredible love and support.

Scene One

(Lights up on **THREE MONKEYS** *who sit staring into the eyes of the audience.)*

(After just long enough...)

MONKEY 1.

OOH OOH OOH OOH

(They listen for a response.)

MONKEY 2.

OOH OOH OOH OOH OOH OOH OOH OOH

(They listen for a response and then laugh uproariously.)

MONKEY 3.

OOH OOH OOH OOH AGH AGH AGH

MONKEY 1 & 2.

OOH OOH OOH OOH AGH AGH AGH

MONKEY 1, 2, & 3.

OOH OOH OOH OOH AGH AGH AGH

(Ooh ooh ooh agh agh agh, monkey chaos. Dancing, rolling jumping around, beating their stomachs in rhythm and waving their arms.)

(A drum beat cuts through the chaos.)

(The **MONKEYS** *stop and listen for the sound.)*

(The drum rhythms increase and **THE LAWS OF THE JUNGLE** *begins.)*

*(***BALOO** *enters. A much more grounded energy than the monkeys who continue to dance wildly and laugh at* **BALOO.**)*

(The music, sounds and movement surround the audience and transport them into the deepest part of the Indian jungle.)

BALOO.

> THESE ARE THE LAWS OF THE JUNGLE
> MANY AND MIGHTY ARE THEY
> YOU MUST FOLLOW THE LAWS OF THE JUNGLE
> FOR THE NUMBER ONE LAW IS OBEY
> FOLLOW THE LAWS OF THE JUNGLE
> LISTEN AS WELL AS YOU CAN
> KILL ONLY FOR FOOD AND SURVIVAL
> AND NEVER, EVER KILL MAN
> NEVER, EVER KILL MAN
>
> *(Offstage – a tiger roars.)*
>
> *(The roar stops the monkeys' laughter and* **BALOO**.*)*
>
> *(The* **MONKEYS** *scatter offstage.)*
>
> KEEP PEACE AND THE LAW OF THE JUNGLE
> WILL PROTECT YOU AND THOSE WHO RUN FREE
> FEAR NOT THE LORDS OF THE JUNGLE
> AND A LORD YOU ONE DAY MAY BE
> FOLLOW THE LAW OF THE JUNGLE
> LISTEN AND NEVER LOOK BACK
> THE STRENGTH OF THE PACK IS THE WOLF
> AND THE STRENGTH OF THE WOLF IS ITS PACK
> ......THE STRENGTH OF THE WOLF IS ITS PACK

Scene Two

(The wolf den, **TABAQUI** *a snoopy busybody of a jackal is lazing around.)*

TABAQUI. Hmmmm, I love this part of the jungle.

(She breathes it in.)

So fresh, so green.

FATHER WOLF. Hhrumph

TABAQUI. The rest of the jungle is all dried up...there's like no food!

FATHER WOLF. You eat too much, Tabaqui.

TABAQUI. Seriously! The rivers are all dried up, the lakes are all like...Uh, where's the water? You'll see. Humans will come here too and you'll see.

FATHER WOLF. You can't blame it all on humans.

TABAQUI. Uh...just did.

RAKSHA. There's a drought.

TABAQUI. Yeah, whatever, ya know...Shere Khan, my great master, he's gonna hunt here now.

FATHER WOLF. He can't! The food on this land is ours!

RAKSHA. Bah, Shere Khan is strong but too slow! He can only catch cattle.

FATHER WOLF. Cattle. Pathetic.

TABAQUI. So should I tell him he's welcome?

FATHER WOLF. You jackals are mischief!

(Offstage – **SHERE KHAN** *roars.)*

Out!

(He growls.)

TABAQUI. I'm going, geez. Touchy, touchy. You can share, ya know.

*(***TABAQUI*** exits.)*

*(***SHERE KHAN*** roars again.)*

FATHER WOLF. Fool! His noise will scare the deer away!

(**RAKSHA** *smells for the scent.*)

RAKSHA. It's not deer he hunts.

(**SHERE KHAN** – *a full throated roar as he misses his kill.*)

He's missed.

FATHER WOLF. Serves him right.

RAKSHA. Something's coming!

(*We hear young* **MOWGLI** *running towards the wolf den. He enters afraid and lost.*)

FATHER WOLF. *(about to leap)* A human! Look! It's a man-cub.

RAKSHA. A man-cub? I've never seen one.

(**RAKSHA** *and* **FATHER WOLF** *carefully get a little closer to* **MOWGLI**.)

So little! So bold!

(*Enter* **SHERE KHAN**, *limping, his paw is wounded.*)

SHERE KHAN. There you are!

(**RAKSHA** *protects* **MOWGLI**.)

FATHER WOLF. Shere Khan.

SHERE KHAN. Give him to me!

FATHER WOLF. We don't take orders –

SHERE KHAN. He's mine! *(suspiciously)* His parents have... Run. Off...

RAKSHA. You're in our part of the jungle now, and by our laws, you will not kill him.

SHERE KHAN. His parents tried to kill me!

RAKSHA. So the child should be punished?!

SHERE KHAN. *(holds out a wounded paw)* Their traps. I'll be lame because of them!

RAKSHA. Then go, lame one! The cub is mine!

SHERE KHAN. Grrrr!!!

RAKSHA. Hunter of cubs. Frog-eater. Fish-killer! Beware. One day this cub will hunt you!

FATHER WOLF. Shere Khan! You know it's dangerous to come between a mother and her cub.

SHERE KHAN. I swear, one day to my teeth he'll come!

RAKSHA. Go!

(**SHERE KHAN** *limps out.*)

FATHER WOLF. Shere Khan will not forget this, Mother.

RAKSHA. We'll keep him safe. He's all alone now.

FATHER WOLF. We must ask the pack, he's not one of us.

RAKSHA. They have to let us keep him. He needs us.

(*to* **MOWGLI** *now*)

Shhh. Be still, little frog. Shhhh.

FATHER WOLF. I know nothing of humans, Raksha. We'll need help. Bagheera. He once lived among men, he knows their ways, he'll make a great protector.

RAKSHA. Then let's ask Bagheera to watch over him until he's strong enough to take care of himself.

FATHER WOLF. And Baloo. He can teach him like he teaches the wolf cubs.

RAKSHA. O Mowgli, Mowgli the Frog, I'll call you. Don't be afraid of Shere Khan, one day you will hunt him, just as he's hunted you.

(*Drums begin.*)

(*Transition:* ***THE LAWS OF THE JUNGLE***)

Scene Three

(**BALOO, MOWGLI, BAGHEERA, TABAQUI** *enter.*)

BALOO.
BECAUSE OF HER AGE AND HER WISDOM,
BECAUSE OF HER BARK AND HER PAW,
AKELA, LEADS THE WOLF PACK

(**AKELA** *enters.*)

ALL.
THE WORD OF AKELA IS LAW.
THE WORD OF AKELA IS LAW

AKELA. I have a request to allow this man-cub into the pack?

BALOO. Yes, Akela. A man-cub. This is Mowgli. He's harmless, unafraid of our jungle.

AKELA. I see.

BALOO. I've agreed to teach him, as I teach the wolves. He'll be my greatest student.

AKELA. Bagheera?

BAGHEERA. His wolf family have asked for my protection –

TABAQUI. A cat? Ha! Go home! On behalf of Shere Khan, I want to say, a man-cub has no place –

AKELA. Hush, Tabaqui!

BAGHEERA. It's an honour –

TABAQUI. Oh, please, he'll die in the winter rains, scorch in the sun. If Shere Khan doesn't kill him first!

BAGHEERA. To kill him will bring shame and fear to the jungle.

AKELA. To kill a human means sooner or later humans will come to kill us. Then everyone in the jungle will suffer.

BALOO. Buh, this little bump. He couldn't kill a horsefly.

TABAQUI. He doesn't belong. He's a human!

BAGHEERA. He'll be a better friend than an enemy when he's grown, Akela. The man-cub is no threat to us if he's taught to think like us, behave like us –

BALOO. We'll be his family.

(*Offstage:* **SHERE KHAN** *roars.*)

(**MOWGLI** *stops, afraid of Shere Khan.*)

BAGHEERA. We hear you, Shere Khan –

TABAQUI. Shere Khan will be our leader one –

AKELA. Enough! Right now, I'm your leader! I make the law! Baloo. Bagheera. Though I'm skeptical, I trust your judgment. You'll be responsible for his actions, so, train him well, for Tabaqui is right about one thing...he is a human.

TABAQUI. You see? I told you! I told you, he's human, I told –

AKELA. The man-cub is one of us!

(*Drum begins.*)

(**AKELA** *exits.*)

(**TABAQUI** *follows* **AKELA** *out.*)

TABAQUI. I– He's one of us? Wait Akela, how?...He can't be– Akela, hold up, Shere Khan...

(*Transition:* **THE LAWS OF THE JUNGLE**)

(*Over the drums we hear the sound of the monkeys in the trees as if they had been listening to all this.*)

Scene Four

(The young **MOWGLI** *begins to run and play and as he does grows into a twelve year-old boy.)*

*(***SHERE KHAN** *lingers in the background and sneaks off.)*

BALOO.

I TEACH HIM THE LAWS OF THE JUNGLE –
AS OLD AND AS TRUE AS THE SKY;
TEN YEARS OLDER, THE MAN-CUB HAS GROWN
TO AN OLD BEAR, HOW SUMMERS DO FLY.

*(***MOWGLI** *is in a pounce position concentrating on a fish.)*

MOWGLI. *(thinking he hears* **SHERE KHAN***)* I hear you Shere Khan!

BALOO. Buh, Mowgli, never mind Shere Khan. Concentrate… "Feet that make no noise, eyes that see in the dark…"

MOWGLI. "Ears that can hear the winds in the lairs, and sharp white teeth!" Rahhhh!

(He leaps at the fish and it swims away.)

Ah, Baloo!

BALOO. *(laughing)* Louder than an elephant's trunk. How can such a little bump make so much noise?

MOWGLI. I'm not a little bump!

BALOO. Right. Sorry, when you're as big as I am you tend to lose perspective.

MOWGLI. Yeah, well, I have perspec-perspec-a-tive.

BALOO. Number one rule, kid: "Be quiet."

MOWGLI. It's hard.

BALOO. Why, even a big ol' bear like me can sneak up on an unsuspecting swimmer!

MOWGLI. They're too fast and my tummy's too empty. Let me climb that nut tree and get some lunch.

BALOO. Buh! Nuts won't make you strong. Look at you, you're all skin and bone. Don't you want to be strong like me?

MOWGLI. Yes. But not as hairy.

BALOO. You're kidding? A fur coat like this? You know what this is worth?

(No answer, **MOWGLI** *shakes his head,* **BALOO** *laughs.)*

Come on kid. Again. I told Bagheera I'd have you strong by spring.

MOWGLI. I'll show Bagheera.

(He boxes **BALOO.***)*

I can fight off an elephant, I can fight off a jackal, I can fight off a big ol' bear –

BALOO. You think so? Well what about an angry tiger?

MOWGLI. Ah, Baloo. You think I can't fight off a tiger with these?

(He flexes his muscles.)

BALOO. Hmmm. Maybe a very, very small one... Come on now, I'll show you one more time, but you must watch very closely.

MOWGLI. But I'm hungry.

BALOO. Mowgli.

MOWGLI. Alright, I'm watching.

*(***BALOO** *gets ready by the river. A* **MONKEY** *appears.* **BALOO** *does not notice the monkey.)*

BALOO. Feet that make no noise...eyes that can see in the dark...

MOWGLI. *(Sees the* **MONKEY***; he's never seen one that close before.)* Huh...

MONKEY 1. *(hushes* **MOWGLI***)* Shhhh.

(Flashes **MOWGLI** *a big monkey grin.)*

*(***MOWGLI** *walks toward the* **MONKEY***.)*

(They circle each other.)

(**MOWGLI** *flexes his muscles.*)

(*The* **MONKEY** *imitates* **MOWGLI**.)

BALOO. Ears that can hear the wind in their lairs...and sharp white teeth.

(**MOWGLI** *lifts his right foot then his left.*)

(*The* **MONKEY** *copies him.*)

(*They both have two feet.*)

MONKEY 1. *(quietly)* Oo oo oo oo.

MOWGLI. Oo oo oo oo.

MONKEY 1. Ee ee ee ee

MOWGLI. Ee ee ee ee.

(*The* **MONKEY** *laughs and dances around,* **MOWGLI** *imitates him.*)

(*seeing his tail*)

You have a tail!

BALOO. Caught ya!

MOWGLI. Baloo, look!

(*The* **MONKEY** *disappears.*)

BALOO. Ha ha! Did you see that, Mowgli? Did you see that?

MOWGLI. *(covering up)* Uhh...yes, Baloo. That was amazing!

BALOO. You think you can do that?

MOWGLI. Of course I can, I...I have the best teacher in the whole jungle.

BALOO. Buh!...It's nothin'.

MOWGLI. Can we eat now?

BALOO. Sure, kid. Lets go find Bagheera.

(**BALOO** *and* **MOWGLI** *exit.*)

(*The* **MONKEY 1** *enters.*)

MONKEY 1. Agh agh agh agh! The man-cub, the man-cub!

(**MONKEY 2 & 3** *enters.*)

MONKEY 2. You saw the man-cub?

MONKEY 1. He's all grown now.

MONKEY 3. He's all grown now?

MONKEY 2. He's all grown now.

MONKEY 1. He has feet just like us, he has arms just like us, he's smart just like –

(forgets)

MONKEY 2. We must tell him he's our brother! We must tell him he's our brother!

MONKEY 3. He can be our leader now. Then all in the jungle will see how smart the monkey people really are.

MONKEY 2. How excellent the monkey people really are!

MONKEY 1. We are excellent! We are excellent! We are –

MONKEY 2. Ooh ooh ooh, aah aah aah!

MONKEY 1, 2, & 3. Ooh ooh ooh, aah aah aah!

(MONKEYS exit.)

(Transition: Music)

Scene Five

(**MOWGLI** *enters, using a bamboo stick as a weapon, pretending he's on the hunt for Shere Khan.*)

MOWGLI. *(roaring like* **SHERE KHAN**) Ha ha! Shere Khan! It's me, Mowgli the frog. Where are you Shere Khan?...I can hear you.

(*pretending* **TABAQUI** *is* **SHERE KHAN**)

Ahaaa! Shere Khan! I found you!

TABAQUI. Uh, excuse me? Do I look like Shere Khan to you?

(**TABAQUI** *struts off.*)

(**BALOO** *continues his lesson with* **MOWGLI**.)

(**BAGHEERA** *sits observing.*)

BALOO. Mowgli! Pay attention. Now, the master words for the hunting people –

MOWGLI. Baloo, we did this already.

BALOO. One day you'll have done everything already and then you'll be forced to start doing things again otherwise you'll have nothing left to do.

(**MOWGLI** *stops.*)

MOWGLI. Huh?

BALOO. Buh, I'm a smart bear. Again, the hunting people...

MOWGLI. *(in the hunting people voice, pretending he is a hunter.)* We be of one blood, you and I.

BALOO. Stand still. Now, the birds.

MOWGLI. Uhhhhh...

(**MOWGLI** *pauses trying to remember.* **BALOO** *taps his temple and then* **MOWGLI**'s *to get him to concentrate. He doesn't know his own strength.*)

BALOO. Concentrate.

(**MOWGLI** *repeats, with a bird-like whistle and flaps around like a bird.*)

MOWGLI. Ow!!…Oh yeah, Illoo! Illoo! We be of one blood, you and I. Illoo! Illoo!

BALOO. *(pats* **MOWGLI** *on the head, lovingly but obviously very hard)* Buh, good boy Mowgli.

MOWGLI. Ow! Not again Baloo!

BAGHEERA. Baloo!

> *(***MOWGLI** *scampers off and continues to play, acting out the capture of Shere Khan.)*

You're too rough. How can his little head carry all your talk?

BALOO. He has to learn Bagheera, that's why I hit him, very softly, when he forgets.

BAGHEERA. Softly! What do you know of softness, old iron feet?

BALOO. The master words will protect him.

BAGHEERA. From you? Just make sure you don't kill him.

> *(***BALOO** *and* **BAGHEERA** *notice* **MOWGLI** *acting like a monkey.)*

BALOO. Mowgli!

> *(***BALOO** *scoops up* **MOWGLI** *and pins him to the ground.)*

Have you been playing with monkeys?

MOWGLI. Uh…Yes…

BAGHEERA. Animals without law, eaters of everything?

MOWGLI. They came down from the trees and were nice to me.

BALOO. Monkeys! Monkeys aren't nice, monkeys have never been nice. Except when they want something. But that's not nice!

MOWGLI. Nicer than you!

BALOO. Mowgli.

MOWGLI. They said I was their brother. Their blood brother.

BAGHEERA. A monkey will say anything.

BALOO. They're crazy, ridiculous –

MOWGLI. – They stand on two feet just like me.

BAGHEERA. The monkeys are not like us.

MOWGLI. They're like me! Let me up, Baloo!

BALOO. We don't drink where the monkeys drink; we don't go where the monkeys go; we don't hunt where they hunt; and we don't die where they die.

MOWGLI. Bagheera, help!

BAGHEERA. They're liars, they're thieves, shameless –

(We hear howling and laughing in the air among the branches.)

MOWGLI. Let me up, Baloo!

BAGHEERA. They're trouble! Do you hear?

*(**BALOO** lets **MOWGLI** up.)*

BALOO. Nice! No one thinks monkeys are nice! You can't trust a monkey!

BAGHEERA. The monkeys are forbidden, Mowgli! Forbidden! Baloo should have warned you.

BALOO. I–I?

*(We see **MONKEYS 1 & 2**. When the **MONKEYS** see that **BAGHEERA** and **BALOO** are not paying attention…)*

MONKEY 1. Psssst!

*(**MOWGLI** sees the **MONKEYS** and out of spite he takes off into the trees with them.)*

BAGHEERA. You're his teacher.

BALOO. Yes, but how could –

BAGHEERA. You need to be more observant –

BALOO. But the monkeys – He's growing up, he –

MONKEY 1 & 2. *(calling out from the trees)*
THERE'S NONE IN THE JUNGLE
SO WISE AND GOOD
AND CLEVER AS THE MONKEY KIND!

(The MONKEYS disappear above.)

BALOO.	BAGHEERA.
Mowgli!	Mowgli, Come back!

BAGHEERA. Now look what you've done!

BALOO. We have to go after him!

(BALOO starts to leave.)

BAGHEERA. At your speed! A wounded cow is faster than you. Think! We need a plan.

(BALOO drops to the ground and wails, rolling around like a porcupine.)

(TABAQUI enters but hides when she sees there's something wrong. She listens.)

BALOO. They'll drop him from the trees. Arrula!

BAGHEERA. Baloo!

BALOO. Put dead bats on my head!

BAGHEERA. Baloo!

BALOO. Roll me into the hives of the wild bees and let them sting me to death. I'm a miserable bear!

BAGHEERA. Baloo!! What would the jungle think if I curled myself up like a porcupine and howled like you're doing?

BALOO. What do I care? He may be dead by now.

(TABAQUI sneaks off.)

BAGHEERA. He's a smart boy and well-taught.

BALOO. Buh, I'm a fool! A big, fat, root-digging fool. Wait!! ...The monkeys fear Kaa the rock snake. She steals young monkeys in the night. She can help. We must get Kaa —

(BALOO goes to exit.)

BAGHEERA. Baloo, wait, she's dangerous —

BALOO. Hurry!

BAGHEERA. Baloo! We should discuss this —

(**BAGHEERA** *follows, running after.*)

Baloo.

(Transition: Music)

Scene Six

(MOWGLI and MONKEYS enter. MONKEY 1 & 2 are jumping about trying to get Mowgli to copy them.)

(During the scene SHERE KHAN enters and watches from behind then exits unnoticed by Mowgli or the Monkeys.)

MONKEY 2.

THERE'S NONE IN THE JUNGLE SO WISE AND GOOD AND CLEVER AS THE MONKEY KIND!!

You'll tell all the jungle.

MONKEY 1. If you want to be our brother, tell all! Everyone! Everything! Now you! Now you!

MOWGLI. There's none in the jungle...

(MONKEY 1 & 2 join in and take over.)

MONKEY 1 & 2. So wise and good and clever and good and clever and good and clever and good and clever and...

MOWGLI. As the monkey kind –

MONKEY 2. Tell all, tell all!

(MONKEY 1 notices MOWGLI has no tail.)

MONKEY 1. Agh Agh Agh Agh! Your tail, brother! We lost your tail! We lost your tail!

MOWGLI. I don't have a tail.

MONKEY 2. You don't?

MONKEY 1. You didn't?

MONKEY 2. You did?

MOWGLI. No, I never had –

MONKEY 2. What? WHAAAT??...

MONKEY 1. Brother, your tail hangs down behind!

MOWGLI. No it doesn't! I don't have a tail!

MONKEY 1 & 2.

OOH OOH OOH THIS IS THE WAY OF THE MONKEY KIND. This is the way of the monkey kind.

(They continue repeating themselves, strutting around and checking out their tails.)

(Enter **RANN** *the Bird, flying overhead.)*

RANN. Illoo, Illoo. Illoo, Illoo.

MOWGLI. Rann! Illoo! Illoo! We be of one blood, you and I!

RANN. *(surprised)* Mowgli! Is that you?! With the monkeys?! Is that wise?

MOWGLI. Mark my trail! Tell Baloo and Bagheera.

MONKEY 1. Never mind! Brother, my tail hangs down behind! To the monkey city!

MOWGLI. Mark my tra-il!

(Exit – **MONKEYS** *and* **MOWGLI.** *)*

RANN. They never go far! They never go far! Always pecking at new things, these monkeys. This time, my eyes tell me, they've pecked down trouble for themselves. I'm right behind you, brother! Illoo! Illoo!

(Exit **RANN.** *)*

*(Transition: **KAA MUSIC**)*

Scene Seven

(**KAA** *hangs from a tree branch, her long body curling down around her.*)

(*Enter* – **BALOO** *and* **BAGHEERA.**)

BAGHEERA. Careful, Baloo! She's always very hungry after she's changed her skin. And her eyes –

BALOO. Buh, I know, I know. Don't look her in the eye.

BAGHEERA. She can charm an animal and leave them helpless.

BALOO. Don't I know it.

BAGHEERA. Be careful!

BALOO. Good hunting, Kaa.

KAA. (*waking up*) Good hunting. Baloo. Bagheera. Sssso-Psshaw!

(**KAA** *falls, the branch breaking.*)

The branches are not what they used to be. Nothing but rotten twigs.

BALOO. Maybe your weight has something to do with it.

KAA. What are you sss-saying???

BALOO. Buh…

BAGHEERA. It's the twigs I'm sure, Kaa.

KAA. Sshmmm – I fell on my last hunt…The noise woke the monkeys. They called me evil names.

BALOO. (*under his breath*) Footless…

BAGHEERA. Evil eye…

BALOO. Yellow earth-worm…

BAGHEERA. Speckled frog…

KAA. Sssss! Have they called me that?

BAGHEERA. They'll say anything, they're shameless.

KAA. Earlier today I heard them dancing on the tree tops –

BAGHEERA. We need your help, Kaa! We're looking for the monkeys.

KAA. Ssss, it can be no sssmall thing that takes two such hunters on the trail of monkeys.

BALOO. Those nut-stealers have stolen our man-cub.

KAA. I heard a man-cub was living with the wolf pack, but I didn't believe it.

BALOO. He's the best and smartest and boldest of man-cubs and, I – we– love him, Kaa.

KAA. Ts! Ts! I've also known what love is.

(Music cue to set up **KAA.** *)*

(bluesy)

There are tales I could te-e-ell, I could te-e-ll, I could te-e-ll...

BAGHEERA & BALOO. KAA!!

(Music out.)

BAGHEERA. Perhaps another night, Kaa. We must move fast. Will you help us? They fear you most of all.

KAA. They have good reason. Aaa-ssp!

(licks her chops)

Now, which way did they go?

BALOO. Buhh...

KAA. You don't know?

BALOO. Buhh...

(Enter **RANN.** *)*

RANN. Hillo! Illo! Up, Up! It's I, Rann! Up, Up! Look up, Baloo!

BALOO. Rann!! Not now!! We have to find –

RANN. Mowgli!

BALOO/BAGHEERA. Mowgli!

RANN. They've taken him to the monkey city!

BALOO. The monkey city!

RANN. I've marked his trail! Follow my lead, follow my lead.

BAGHEERA. A full stomach and a deep sleep to you, Rann!

RANN. It's nothing. Nothing at all.

KAA. I'll go on ahead. I'm faster. Besides, I'm starving and they called me footless.

RANN. This way, Kaa!

(Exit RANN *and* KAA.*)*

BALOO. Not the monkey city.

BAGHEERA. Quickly, Baloo!

BALOO. I hate the monkey city.

(They exit.)

*(Transition: **MUSIC OF THE MONKEYS**)*

Scene Eight

(The **MONKEYS** *are dancing and celebrating with* **MOWGLI**.*)*

MONKEY 1. *(with all the* **MONKEYS** *and* **MONKEY KING**)
HERE WE SIT IN OUR BRANCHY KINGDOM,
THINKING OF THINGS WE CAN DO LIKE A HUMAN;

MONKEY 2.
WE'LL RULE THE JUNGLE NOW WE HAVE OUR BROTHER,
EXCELLENTNESS! ONE MAN TO ANOTHER.

MONKEY 3.
LIKE HUMAN'S WE'LL BE ALL WISE AND GOOD,
DONE BY MERELY THINKING WE COULD.
SOMETHING'S MISSING, BUT NEVER MIND

MONKEY 1, 2, & 3.
BROTHER, YOUR TAIL HANGS DOWN BEHIND!

(The **MONKEYS** *carry on with their laughter and dancing.)*

MOWGLI. I've told you a million times! I don't have a tail!

MONKEY 1. I found your tail, brother!

MONKEY 2. Your tail! Your tail!

*(***MONKEY 1** *grabs a vine, ties it around* **MOWGLI***'s waist like a tail, and whips him back into the dance.)*

MOWGLI. Whoaaa!

MONKEY KING.
ALL THE TALK WE EVER HAVE HEARD
UTTERED BY BAT OR BEAST OR BIRD –
HUMANS ARE MADE WITH MINDS THAT ARE BETTER –
NOW WITH YOU, WE'RE ALL THINKING TOGETTER!
EXCELLENT! EXCELLENT! ONCE AGAIN!
NOW WE'LL BE TALKING JUST LIKE MEN!

MONKEY 1.
BUT BROTHER THAT'S NOT A REAL...

MONKEY KING.
AH NEVER MIND,

ALL MONKEYS.
> BROTHER, YOUR TAIL HANGS DOWN BEHIND!

MONKEY KING.
> THIS IS THE WAY OF THE MONKEY-KIND.

ALL MONKEYS.
> THIS IS THE WAY OF THE MONKEY-KIND.

MONKEY KING.
> THERE IS NONE IN THE JUNGLE SO WISE AND GOOD
> AND CLEVER AS THE MONKEY-KIND!

ALL MONKEYS.
> OOH OOH AGH AGH OOH OOH AGH AGH AGH AGH!

MONKEY KING. *(like Elvis)* Uh, thank you, uh, thank you very much.

ALL MONKEYS. *(laughing and clapping)* Oo-oo-ah-ah-ah-ah!!!

MONKEY KING. *(to MOWGLI)* Welcome to our kingdom, our brother.

MOWGLI. Thank you...

MONKEY KING. *(pointing out his crown)* Majesty.

MOWGLI. Majesty?

MONKEY KING. That's right! Majesty! I'm the Majesty.

MONKEY 1. He's the Majesty.

MONKEY 2. The Majesty. Majesty.

MONKEY 3. I like Majesty.

MONKEY KING. Now, as our new brother, you'll teach us everything we need to know to be most excellent humans.

MONKEY 3. Oh yes, most excellent!

ALL MONKEYS. Most excellent humans!!!!

MOWGLI. Humans, Majesty?

MONKEY KING. You are human, aren't you?

MOWGLI. I'm a wolf.

> *(The MONKEYS laugh at MOWGLI who is obviously not a wolf.)*

MONKEY KING. A wolf?! A wolf has four legs, fur, pointy teeth, ears. No, no, I'm most positive you're a human.

MOWGLI. Only on the outside, Majesty. I'm more wolf than human.

MONKEY KING. More wolf than human? Ha!

(to the **MONKEYS**)

That's funny.

MONKEY 2. Funny, funny, very funny.

MONKEY 1. Wolf-human! He's a wolf-human!

MONKEY KING. Wolf-human or not, you're still human and you will teach us to be humans too.

MONKEY 3. And tell all in the jungle how excellent we really are.

MONKEY 1. Everyone in the jungle, all about our most excellent selves.

MONKEY 2 & 3. Our excellent selves! Our excellent selves!

MOWGLI. I'll tell them, but I don't think anyone's going to believe me.

MONKEY KING. Believe you?! But you're human, you're most excellent.

MONKEY 2. You are most excellent.

MONKEY KING. Why??? Why! Why would they not believe you?

MOWGLI. Uhm, well, Baloo says you're all crazy.

MONKEY 1. Who Baloo? Baloo who?

MONKEY 2. Baloo who? Baloo who?

MONKEY KING. We're not crazy! We're excellent!!! We're excellent! Why crazy? Why crazy?

MOWGLI. You have no laws. No hunting call, nothing but silly words –

MONKEY KING. Words, laws, my brother! My brother, you are going to make our laws.

MOWGLI. I have to go home.

MONKEY KING. Home? Brother, this is your home!

MONKEY 1. You're home, Brother! You're home!

(**MONKEY 1** *ties up* **MOWGLI** *and ties his tail to a tree.*)

MOWGLI. Um, what are you doing?

MONKEY KING. You are going to be our leader!

MOWGLI. Bagheera wouldn't like that very much.

MONKEY KING. I would like that! I would like that!

(**MONKEY 1, 2 & 3** *begin to swing.*)

MONKEY 1, 2, & 3. We would like that! We would like that! We are excellent, we are excellent!

(*Enter –* **SHERE KHAN***, roar.*)

(**MONKEY 1** *lets go in fear and* **MONKEY 2** *flies offstage just missing* **SHERE KHAN***.*)

MONKEY 2. Excelleeeeeee-nnnnn–t!

MONKEY 1 & 2. Hee hee hee...oops!

SHERE KHAN. There you are...you ran off, just like your parents.

MONKEY KING. Shere Khan! How nice of you to join our party!

MOWGLI. *(terrified)* Hhh! We be of one blood, you and I!

MONKEY 1, 3 & MONKEY KING. *(laughing and dancing around)* We be of one blood! We be of one blood!

MOWGLI. Help me!!

SHERE KHAN. Thank you my monkey friends for taking such good care of my little man-cub.

MONKEY 1. We did? We were?

MONKEY 3. We what?

SHERE KHAN. There is none in the jungle so wise –

(**MONKEYS** *join in, beginning to dance again, laughing, distracted.*)

MONKEY 1, 3 & MONKEY KING. – and good and clever as the monkey kind!!! The monkey kind! The monkey kind!

(*In the excitement* **MONKEY 3** *gets swung offstage.*)

MONKEY 1 & MONKEY KING. Oooh, ooh, ooh, agh agh agh....

(noticing **MONKEY 3** *is gone)*

Oops!

SHERE KHAN. *(watching them with judgment)* Yes...Well...Until then allow me to say, that it will be known throughout the jungle how excellent you monkeys truly are...

MONKEY KING. Oh Shere Khan, we truly are, most excellent. Most excellent!

SHERE KHAN. Right...Now, you will come with me my little frog.

MONKEY KING. Actually, uh...Shere Khan, he's not a frog, he's a human.

SHERE KHAN. RRRReally?

MONKEY KING. Oh yeah. He thinks he's a wolf. Ha! I mean look at him. Ha! Obviously human!

MONKEY 1. He's a real live human!

MONKEY KING. He's our brother, and our most excellent leader.

SHERE KHAN. Your leaderrrr?

MONKEY KING. I know. He's ours! Our leader. Isn't that excellent?

MONKEY 1. It's excellent! Very excell –

SHERE KHAN. *(angry)* NO!

MONKEY 1. Not excellent.

SHERE KHAN. THE MAN-CUB IS MINE!

MONKEY KING. ...Of course he is. We knew that didn't we?

MONKEY 1. Didn't we?

MONKEY KING. Didn't we. Take him away, Shere Khan. Take him away. With no tail the cub can't swing! The cub can't swing!

(The **MONKEYS** *give a tied up* **MOWGLI** *to* **SHERE KHAN.***)*

MONKEY 1. The cub can't swing! The cub can't sawwwwing-aaa! AGH, AGH AGH!

*(***SHERE KHAN** *purrs and goes towards* **MOWGLI.***)*

MOWGLI. Wait! You said I was your brother! Help! We be of one....

(**KAA** *enters, coming between* **MOWGLI** *and* **SHERE KHAN.**)

KAA. One blood you and I!

MONKEY 1 & MONKEY KING. Kaa! It's Kaa! Kaa!

KAA. Ssssstop where you are!

(**SHERE KHAN** *and the* **MONKEYS** *stop in their tracks.*)

MONKEY 1. Her eyes! Her eyes! Don't look at them. Don't look at them!...I'm looking at them.

KAA. Sssshere Khan.

SHERE KHAN. Kaa.

KAA. I wasn't exssspecting you. Pleassse, Sssstay for sssssupper!

SHERE KHAN. *(knowing he can't beat* **KAA***)* I swear one day to my teeth you'll come, Man-cub!

(**SHERE KHAN** *angrily exits.*)

MONKEY 1. I'm still looking at them. I'm still looking at them!

(**KAA** *hypnotizes* **MONKEY 1** *and the* **MONKEY KING.**)

KAA.

THISSS IS THE HOUR OF PRIDE AND POWER,
TALON, TAIL AND CLAW.
You cannot ssstir foot or hand! Sspeak!

KAA & MONKEYS.

THISSS ISSS THE HOUR OF PRIDE AND POWER,
TALON, TAIL AND CLAW.

KAA. Let the chassse begin! Boo!

(*As* **KAA** *fakes an attack, the* **MONKEYS** *scream and exit.*)

(**KAA** *goes to* **MOWGLI.**)

Ssssoo you are the man-cub!

MOWGLI. *(not wanting to look in to her eyes)* I'm Mowgli. Mowgli of the wolf pack.

KAA. You're in a ssssticky sssituation, aren't you man-cub. Sssss, you're not unlike the monkeyssssss.

MOWGLI. They think they're human, and excellent. Most excellent.

KAA. Very annoying, yessss?

MOWGLI. Yesss. I know I stand on two feet like they do, but that tail makes them do crazy things.

KAA. Yesss, you're quite right.

(Due to her constrictor instincts **KAA** *begins to circle* **MOWGLI**.*)*

MOWGLI. We be of one blood, you and I. My kill shall be your kill if you're ever hungry, Kaa.

KAA. Ssssank you.

MOWGLI. I have skill in these, *(He holds out his hands.)* if you're in trouble I can help you.

(Enter **BALOO** *and* **BAGHEERA**.*)*

BALOO/BAGHEERA. Mowgli!!

(seeing **KAA***)*

KAA!!

*(***BALOO** *grabs* **KAA***'s tail to stop her from squeezing* **MOWGLI**.*)*

KAA. Sssorry, inssstinct!

BALOO. Are you hurt, little brother?

MOWGLI. I'm ok.

BALOO. You're safe.

BAGHEERA. For now.

MOWGLI. Kaa put a charm on the monkeys and made them run away. Even Shere Khan was afraid.

BAGHEERA. Shere Khan? He was here? You owe Kaa your life.

(to **KAA***)*

Thank you, Kaa.

KAA. My pleasssssure. Sssssuppertime!

(KAA slithers off.)

BALOO. You see where playing with monkeys gets you.

MOWGLI. You were right, Baloo. I'm sorry. I shouldn't have run off like that.

BAGHEERA. You may not be so lucky next time. I must give this some thought, Mowgli...But for now...

BALOO. Buh, let's go home.

(They exit.)

(Transition: Music.)

Scene Nine

(**TABAQUI** *is relaxing on a rock.*)

(**MOWGLI** *walks slowly towards* **TABAQUI**, *trying to hypnotise her like Kaa did to the monkeys.*)

(**BAGHEERA** *watches him closely.*)

MOWGLI. Thissss issss the hour of pride and power. Talon, tail and claw. Sssss, You can not sssstir foot or hand. Ssssspea –

TABAQUI. Man-cub. What are you doing?

MOWGLI. What do you thhhhhink I am doing?

TABAQUI. I'm not ssssure, but ya look pretty sssstupid.

MOWGLI. (*frustrated*) What am I doing, I'm not a snake.

(*trying to find his confidence*)

I'm a wolf!

(*He gets on all fours and starts growling at* **TABAQUI**.)

Grrrrr rarrrrr!

(*Offstage –* **SHERE KHAN** *roars.*)

(**MOWGLI** *stops.*)

TABAQUI. Careful man-cub. Caaarrefulll! If you haven't noticed, your fearless leader, Akela is an old wolf. She'll miss her kill soon, and you know what that means? Without her as your leader, your time in the jungle is done.

MOWGLI. That'll never happen. I'm part of the pack.

TABAQUI. You're still human!

MOWGLI. (*on all fours like a wolf*) I'm a wolf.

(**MOWGLI** *jumps at* **TABAQUI**.)

BAGHEERA. (*who has watched all this*) Mowgli! You're human.

MOWGLI. The wolves are my brothers.

BAGHEERA. Yes, but you're still human. One day you may want to meet other humans.

TABAQUI. If Shere Khan doesn't eat ya first.

(BAGHEERA leaps towards TABAQUI and she exits.)

MOWGLI. Bagheera? Why does Shere Khan want to kill me?

BAGHEERA. Because you're human.

MOWGLI. *(sullenly)* Just because I'm human?

BAGHEERA. We in the jungle have learned to never under-estimate the power of man. You hold great power in those hands of yours. The power to love and mend but also the power to destroy, and kill. Shere Khan is afraid.

MOWGLI. Afraid?

BAGHEERA. Afraid every human is the same. That every human will try to destroy our home. That every human will set his trap.

MOWGLI. *(shakes his head)* So he wants to kill me? Hm, what does Tabaqui know? I have you and Baloo to protect me.

BAGHEERA. We can't be there every time, Mowgli.

MOWGLI. I know.

BAGHEERA. It's time. My thinking is done. You're growing up, you're stronger. You must learn to protect yourself.

MOWGLI. How?

BAGHEERA. Go to the human village. Find the red flower that grows there.

MOWGLI. The red flower?

BAGHEERA. Animals fear it. It's very very dangerous but very powerful. It will keep you safe.

MOWGLI. The red flower, that grows in the village. Let's go.

BAGHEERA. No Mowgli, you must go alone.

MOWGLI. Alone?....

(BAGHEERA nods.)

I'll go Bagheera! I'll go!

BAGHEERA. Be careful, Mowgli.

MOWGLI. I will.

*(Transition: Music segue into **SONG OF THE RED FLOWER.**)*

(The lullaby [SONG OF THE RED FLOWER] starts
MOWGLI *off on his journey and shows his capture of the*
red flower.)

(It is night by the time **MOWGLI** *gets to the human vil-*
lage. From a distance **MOWGLI** *watches a human with*
the fire. He sees how he tends it. He lights a torch. Once
the human has left, **MOWGLI** *takes the torch. He feels*
its heat when he gets too close. He sneaks away with it.)

SONG OF THE RED FLOWER

RAKSHA.

ON THE TRAIL THAT YOU MUST TREAD
WHERE THE FLOWER BLOSSOMS RED.
WOOD AND WATER, WIND AND TREE
JUNGLE-FAVOUR GO WITH THEE
THROUGH THE DAY AND THROUGH THE NIGHT,
GUARD MY CUB FROM HARM AND FRIGHT.
WOOD AND WATER, WIND AND TREE,
JUNGLE-FAVOUR GO WITH THEE!

(add **MOWGLI***)*

WOOD AND WATER, WIND AND TREE
JUNGLE-FAVOUR GO WITH ME (THEE)

Scene Ten

(**BALOO** and **BAGHEERA** are pacing.)

BALOO. He should be back by now.

BAGHEERA. Well, he's not.

BALOO. Buh, but he should be.

BAGHEERA. Well he's not.

BALOO. (a long pause) Buhhhh, I can't stand it any longer. I should have gone with him. They got him, Shere Khan got him.

BAGHEERA. Baloo.

BALOO. I should have gone!

(**TABAQUI** enters.)

BAGHEERA. He needs to learn to do things on his own. He needs –

(They stop at the sight of **TABAQUI**.)

TABAQUI. What?…Good hair day?!

BALOO. Tabaqui.

TABAQUI. You're wanted at council rock.

BALOO. Says who?

TABAQUI. Uh…Me! Akela's missed her kill. Bye bye, Akela, hello, Shere Khan! He'll lead the pack now.

BAGHEERA. That's for the pack to decide.

TABAQUI. So…where's our little man-cub?…He's been gone quite sometime. We wouldn't want to disappoint Shere Khan. He's expecting him.

BALOO. Arullla! Mouth shut, Tabaqui!

TABAQUI. Touchy…touchy…

BAGHEERA. Shere Khan should tread carefully.

BALOO. Jungle law. Never kill man.

TABAQUI. Never kill man! Why? 'Cause man would never kill us? Please.

BALOO. Tabaqui! You're makin' my whiskers twitch.

TABAQUI. Okay, okay, I got it already, geesh!

(*TABAQUI exits.*)

(**BALOO** *and* **BAGHEERA** *share a knowing silence.*)

(**MOWGLI** *enters.*)

MOWGLI. Rahhhrr!

BALOO.	**BAGHEERA.**
Mowgli! You made it!	Mowgli!!

(**BALOO** *rushes towards him.*)

MOWGLI. Careful, Baloo. Look!

(**MOWGLI** *shows them the red flower.*)

BALOO. The red flower!

BAGHEERA. Well done, little brother.

(**BALOO** *gets too close and burns his whiskers.*)

BALOO. Bahowwe!

BAGHEERA. Baloo!

MOWGLI. I said be careful. It's very hot!

BAGHEERA. Mowgli. Akela has missed her kill. A new leader will be chosen. Many want Shere Khan's protection.

MOWGLI. From what? We don't need it, Bagheera. We have the red flower. Let's go.

(*drum beat*)

BAGHEERA. Mowgli, you must be careful.

(*They exit.*)

(*Transition:* ***SHERE KHAN MUSIC***)

Scene Eleven

(**SHERE KHAN** and **TABAQUI** talk to the pack/audience.)

TABAQUI. Animals of the jungle! The laws of the jungle must change! With my lord, Shere Khan, as your new leader there will be no fear of hunger, no fear of danger, no fear of humans!!

SHERE KHAN.
WHO IS YOUR HUNTER, HUNTER BOLD

TABAQUI.
MY LORD! THOUGH THE HUNT MAY BE LONG AND COLD

SHERE KHAN.
WHO WILL LEAD THE HUNGRY TOWARDS THE KILL?

TABAQUI.
MY LORD! LEAD US SHERE KHAN OF THE JUNGLE, YOU WILL

SHERE KHAN.
WHO HOLDS THE POWER THAT WILL MAKE OUR PRIDE

TABAQUI.
MY LORD! WE'LL FOREVER STAND BY YOUR SIDE
MY LORD! WE'LL FOREVER STAND BY YOUR SIDE

SHERE KHAN. Thank you, Tabaqui.

TABAQUI. Anytime, Shere Khan. You know I've been thinking –

SHERE KHAN. Tabaqui!

TABAQUI. Mm hmm.

SHERE KHAN. You're done.

TABAQUI. Yup.

SHERE KHAN. Wolves! The jungle is home to the animals. It is our rightful home. Humans do not belong here, they have drained our lakes, dried up our rivers, stolen our food, stolen our land, stolen our freedom!

TABAQUI. Shere Khan! She comes, she comes, the old wolf comes...

(**AKELA** enters.)

AKELA. My pack. I'm an old wolf…I've missed my kill. By jungle law, you have the right to choose a new leader –

SHERE KHAN. – Ah, The leadership is now open, and having been asked to speak –

*(***MOWGLI, BALOO,*** and ***BAGHEERA*** enter.)*

MOWGLI. By whom? What place has a tiger among our pack?

BAGHEERA. Mowgli.

TABAQUI. Yeah okay, "man-cub!"

MOWGLI. You don't know our ways. You don't follow our laws.

SHERE KHAN. Laws change. Humans don't belong in the jungle. Can't you see what they've done?

BAGHEERA. He's not like all humans as you are not like all animals.

SHERE KHAN. Ragh –

AKELA. He's part of our pack. Our brother, in all but blood!

SHERE KHAN. He's a man, a man's child, and from the marrow of my bones…

(to **MOWGLI***)*

I hate you!

MOWGLI. My brothers, you can't take Shere Khan as your leader. He hates me only for being human. But I'm a wolf, just like you. I'm just like you.

SHERE KHAN. *(laughing at* **MOWGLI***)* "I'm just like you." Enough "man-cub." They've seen what your kind can do.

MOWGLI. I'm your brother.

SHERE KHAN. Does he look like your brother? Does he look like a wolf?

MOWGLI. *(pulling out the fire)* I'm more of a wolf than you'll ever be!

BAGHEERA. Mowgli!

SHERE KHAN. Hmmm, a wolf, you say. But I thought wolves were afraid of the red flower.

(He looks out to the wolf pack.)

Oh look, I was right. I'm sure he didn't mean to scare you. Bagheera, did you forget to tell him?

MOWGLI. Don't be afraid. This will keep us safe. I'll keep us safe.

SHERE KHAN. *(laughing)* You? You'll keep them safe? A pack of wolves. Are you going to lead them now too? You and your "red flower?" You a "man-cub?" A man –

MOWGLI. I'm not a man – !

*(**MOWGLI** thrusts the fire towards **SHERE KHAN**, burning him.)*

*(**SHERE KHAN** roars and runs off in fear.)*

TABAQUI. *(following after **SHERE KHAN**)* Shere Khan! Shere Khan!

MOWGLI. *(looking at the fire)* What...

*(**MOWGLI** looks out to his brothers.)*

My brothers. Please. Don't go. I didn't mean – I don't want you to be afraid. I didn't...Shere Khan, he... Please. Don't go. Please, I'm your brother...I'm –

(He looks at the fire again, not knowing what to do.)

I'll go...I'll go to the human village...Where a man-cub should live. But you'll always be my brothers. And Akela will always be my leader.

*(**MOWGLI** weeps.)*

What did I do? What is it? What's this water in my eyes? Am I dying, Baloo?

*(**BALOO** goes to **MOWGLI**.)*

BALOO. No Mowgli, they're only tears, let them fall.

MOWGLI. I'm sorry Bagheera, I didn't mean to...

BAGHEERA. I know Mowgli, I know.

*(Enter **RAKSHA**.)*

RAKSHA. Mowgli.

MOWGLI. Mother!

RAKSHA. I'm sorry, my little frog.

MOWGLI. The jungle is afraid of me, I don't belong here anymore, I have to leave.

RAKSHA. Oh, Mowgli.

MOWGLI. I don't want to go, but Shere Khan –

RAKSHA. I'm not afraid of Shere Khan, don't you be. Be brave, Mowgli. I love you.

MOWGLI. I love you, Mother.

(turning to **BALOO** *and* **BAGHEERA***)*

Good bye, Baloo. Good bye, Bagheera.

BALOO. You can't just go.

MOWGLI. I have to.

(He starts to leave.)

Don't forget me.

BALOO. I won't forget you, kid. Good bye, little bump.

*(***MOWGLI*** runs off.)*

We can't just let him go like that.

BAGHEERA. He has to figure it out on his own, Baloo. He has to realize what he's done.

BALOO. Yeah. Yeah, I thought you'd say that.

(Transition music: **SONG OF THE RED FLOWER***)*

RAKSHA.

WOOD AND WATER, WIND AND TREE,
JUNGLE-FAVOUR GO WITH THEE!

Scene Twelve

(**TABAQUI** *runs on to find* **SHERE KHAN** *licking his wounds.*)

TABAQUI. Shere Khan! Shere Khan!

SHERE KHAN. Find him, Tabaqui. I'm going to make sure that man-cub never returns to this jungle.

TABAQUI. Well, he said he was going to live in the human village so I mean, you got nothing to worry about –

SHERE KHAN. Find him! Tell me exactly where he is. And if you don't, Tabaqui, your days in the jungle will be over too.

TABAQUI. Uh...Shere Khan –

SHERE KHAN. GO!!

TABAQUI. *(startled)* Okay. Okay. I'm going.

(**TABAQUI** *howls and follows* **MOWGLI**.)

(*Transition: Music segue into* ***HE HURRIES ON***.)

(**MOWGLI** *begins his journey as* **TABAQUI** *follows behind.*)

MOWGLI.

THE PATH IS ROUGH AS I RUN THROUGH THE TREES

TABAQUI.

HE HURRIES – HE HURRIES ON

MOWGLI.

I COME TO A VALLEY, SHELTERED FROM THE BREEZE

TABAQUI.

HE HURRIES – HE HURRIES ON

MOWGLI.

THE VALLEY OPENS OUT INTO A GREAT WIDE PLAIN

TABAQUI.

HE HURRIES – HE HURRIES ON

MOWGLI.

I SEE BUFFALOES GRAZING AS I RUN THROUGH THE RAIN

TABAQUI.

HE HURRIES – HE HURRIES ON

MOWGLI.

I SEE A HUMAN VILLAGE THROUGH THE MISTY HAZE

TABAQUI.

HE HURRIES – HE HURRIES ON

*(***TWO VILLAGERS*** appear.)*

MOWGLI.

THE VILLAGERS WATCH ME, STUNNED AND AMAZED

*(They stop and stare at ***MOWGLI***.)*

*(***TABAQUI*** watches in the distance.)*

*(***MOWGLI*** tries to communicate with the humans.)*

We be of one blood you and I!

*(The ***HUMANS*** look at one another.)*

*(***MOWGLI*** flexes his muscles at them as with the monkeys.)*

*(The ***HUMANS*** look at each other.)*

*(***MOWGLI*** lifts his legs, one and two.)*

(The humans look confused.)

We – be – of – one – blood – you – and – I...

*(The ***HUMANS*** converse with one another in gibberish. ***MOWGLI*** doesn't understand.)*

*(Through movement ***MOWGLI*** tries to explain that he lives with the wolves, he grew up with the wolves, and he himself is actually a wolf.)*

*(The ***HUMANS*** back away, afraid of ***MOWGLI***'s animalistic behavior.)*

I'm Mowgli, the frog. Mowgli the frog, they call me!

*(***MOWGLI*** cannot understand the humans and the frustration gets to him.)*

Mowgli, of the wolf pack!

*(The ***HUMANS*** exit, confused and slightly afraid.)*

*(***MOWGLI*** sits down by the fire defeated.)*

*(***TABAQUI*** looks around, watches ***MOWGLI***, about to go to him but instead runs off.)*

MOWGLI. *(cont.)* I want to go home.

(**MOWGLI** *hears his mother's lullaby.*)

RAKSHA.

WOOD AND WATER, WIND AND TREE
JUNGLE-FAVOUR GO WITH THEE
JUNGLE-FAVOUR GO WITH THEE

(**MOWGLI** *stokes the fires and lies down to rest.*)

Scene Thirteen

(**BALOO** *and* **BAGHEERA** *sit sullenly, deep in thought.*)

(**TABAQUI** *enters.*)

TABAQUI. So...just thought you should know that the man-cub may be in a little bit o' trouble.

BALOO. Tabaqui, go home.

TABAQUI. Yup, I'm serious. Shere Khan knows where he is. He's waiting for him in the ravine outside the village.

BAGHEERA. Tabaqui, if you're lying...!

TABAQUI. I'm not! Okay?

(*assuring them*)

I'm not. He's going to kill him.

BALOO. Go, Bagheera. I'll tell Akela and catch up.

(**BAGHEERA** *exits.*)

TABAQUI. (*calling after* **BAGHEERA**) Ya didn't hear it from me!

(**BALOO** *looks at* **TABAQUI.**)

What?...

BALOO. Thanks, Tabaqui.

(**BALOO** *exits.*)

TABAQUI. Yeah, yeah. It'd be nice if someone wanted to save me one o' these days.

Scene Fourteen

(**MOWGLI** *sleeps by the fire.*)

(**BAGHEERA** *quietly enters.*)

BAGHEERA. *(whispers)* Mowgli. Mowgli.

MOWGLI. Bagheera! What are you doing here?

BAGHEERA. Listen Mowgli, we don't have much time, Shere Khan –

MOWGLI. – I didn't mean to hurt him, Bagheera –

BAGHEERA. – He's embarrassed and very angry. Tabaqui told us he's waiting for you in the ravine at the edge of the village.

MOWGLI. Tabaqui? Ah, she's always making trouble –

BAGHEERA. Not this time, Mowgli. Jungle law says you must protect yourself. You must kill Shere Khan. Before he kills you.

MOWGLI. Kill…I can't, Bagheera.

BAGHEERA. He's given you no choice.

MOWGLI. I can't.

BAGHEERA. We'll help you.

(*Enter* **AKELA** *and* **BALOO** *out of breath.*)

BALOO. Mowgli!

MOWGLI. Baloo!

BALOO. Bawe, I missed you, kid.

MOWGLI. I missed you too, Baloo!

AKELA. Mowgli! I have a plan. Bagheera and I will take the buffalo pack to the edge of the ravine. You and Baloo find Shere Khan. On your command, we'll charge the buffalo into the ravine.

BAGHEERA. Shere Khan will be trapped.

BALOO. Ready, Mowgli?

MOWGLI. *(nods)* …

AKELA. Let's go!

(**BAGHEERA** *and* **AKELA** *go one way and* **BALOO** *and* **MOWGLI** *the other.*)

(*Transition: the drums begin.*)

Scene Fifteen

(**MOWGLI** *and* **BALOO** *stand on the edge of the ravine.*)

MOWGLI. I'm scared, Baloo.

BALOO. Be strong, little bump. We'll be going home soon.

(**MOWGLI** *looks down into the ravine.*)

(**TABAQUI** *slyly enters and watches in the distance.*)

MOWGLI. Shere Khan! I see him, Baloo! Down there. In the ravine, just like Tabaqui said.

(Finding the courage, he calls to **SHERE KHAN**.*)*

Shere Khan! Shere Khan! It's me, Mowgli the frog! Mowgli of the wolf pack! Do you hear me, Shere Khan?

SHERE KHAN. Man-cub.

MOWGLI. I know why you're here Shere Khan. Please. Let me live freely in the jungle. Where I belong.

BALOO. Mowgli.

MOWGLI. With my brothers, my family, my pack!

SHERE KHAN. *(roars)* Never!!

BALOO. Now, Mowgli!

MOWGLI. Alalalalalalala!

BALOO. There they go!

MOWGLI. Down! Hurry!

BALOO. The buffalo, Mowgli! Look. Look at them run down the sides of the ravine.

MOWGLI. Where's Bagheera?

BALOO. There he is. Leading them in. There's Akela on the other side.

MOWGLI. Shere Khan! Look at his eyes, Baloo.

BALOO. It's okay, Mowgli. The ravine walls are too high, the buffalo are too fast.

MOWGLI. There's no way out.

BALOO. He's trapped.

MOWGLI. There's hundreds of them.

BALOO. Look at them run –

MOWGLI. – So fast –

BALOO. Hundreds of them, over top of Shere Khan –

MOWGLI. I can't see him anymore –

BALOO. Hundreds of them.

MOWGLI. I can't see…He's gone…

BALOO. The buffalo were too fast. He couldn't escape. He'll never come after you again. It's all over, little bump. You're free.

MOWGLI. I'm free.

(silence)

I, Mowgli, am free…My heart is sad, from the things I don't understand.

BALOO. The ways of the jungle are not always easy.

MOWGLI. The humans didn't understand me at all, they were afraid of me.

BAGHEERA. Not of you. Of what they didn't know, of what they didn't understand.

MOWGLI. I promise to never put the jungle in danger again. I want to come home. I want to live with you in the jungle. I don't belong in the human village. I'm not like them, I'm like you. I belong with you. You're my family. My home….

AKELA. Mowgli. You will always be one of us. Wherever your journeys may take you, your home will always be here.

MOWGLI. Thank you, Akela.

*(sees **TABAQUI**)*

Hey, Tabaqui. Thanks.

TABAQUI. Yeah yeah, don't get all, "Thank you for saving my life" on me.

(hears her stomach)

Whoa! Did you hear that? My stomach. I gotta eat, who's got somethin', anything…

(to a kid in the audience)

Hey, kid, you gonna eat that, kid.

BALOO. Buh…let's go home, Mowgli. Where you belong…
So what if you're not as hairy as the rest of us.

BAGHEERA. Give him time, Baloo, Give him time.

MOWGLI. He's only kidding. Right, Bagheera? Right,
Bagheera?

BALOO. Remember, Mowgli…

*(Transition: **THE LAWS OF THE JUNGLE**)*

REMEMBER THE LAW OF THE JUNGLE
REMEMBER AND NEVER LOOK BACK
THE STRENGTH OF THE PACK IS THE WOLF,
AND THE STRENGTH OF ONE WOLF IS ITS PACK.
THIS IS THE LAW OF THE JUNGLE
AS OLD AND AS TRUE AS THE SKY
THE FAMILY YOU'VE GIVEN YOUR LOVE TO
IS THE FAMILY WHO'LL STAND BY YOUR SIDE

The End

Song of the Red Flower

Tracey Power